I Want to Be A FIRE FIGHTER

By Linda Lee Maifair
Illustrated by Tom Cooke

A SESAME STREET/GOLDEN PRESS BOOK
Published by Western Publishing Company, Inc.,
in conjunction with Children's Television Workshop.

 Library of Congress Catalog Card Number: 91-70830 ISBN: 0-307-12626-9/ISBN: 0-307-62626-1 (lib. bdg.) MCMXCII

My uncle Grady is a fire fighter. Today is his birthday. Mommy baked a cake to surprise him.

"I will surprise Uncle Grady, too," I told my mommy. "I, Grover, will dress up like a fire fighter."

Mommy told me that fire fighters wear helmets to protect themselves when they fight fires.

I found this hat in a trunk up in the attic. It looks like a fire fighter's helmet.

Mommy said fire fighters need special masks and air tanks because it is very difficult to breathe in smoky buildings.

I went to my room and put on my catcher's mask. Then I looked for something that would help me breathe in a smoky building. Aha! I found the perfect thing.

Mommy told me that fire fighters use swooshing water from big hoses to put out fires. They wear rubber raincoats and tall rubber boots to keep dry.

Oh, look! Here is my old slicker. It still fits me. And Grandpa's fishing boots are very tall!

I could not wait for Uncle Grady to see me, Grover, in a fire fighter's outfit. I ran to answer the door.

"Surprise!" we both said at the same time. Uncle Grady was wearing his fire fighter's outfit, too! He wore it just for me. He calls it his turnout gear.

"Grover," he said, "you look like a real fire fighter! Would you like to go with me to the firehouse?"

"Oh, yes, please," I said.

When we got there, nobody was home. "Oh, my goodness," I said to Uncle Grady. "A very big family must live here. They have gone out to play in the middle of dinner."

"A squad of fire fighters is like a family, Grover," Uncle Grady said. "They live and work together many hours a day. But they have not gone out to play. When the alarm sounds, fire fighters have to stop whatever they are doing and race to the fire."

Then we went upstairs. "This is where we spend time when we are not out fighting a fire," said Uncle Grady.

"When I am a fire fighter, I will sleep here, too," I said. "I hope I can bring my Teddy Monster."

"I will show you how fire fighters get down to the garage when the alarm goes off in the middle of the night. We jump out of our beds and into our gear. Then we slide down this pole, right through a hole in the floor."

Wow! It was a long way down.

"Come on!" Uncle Grady said. "The fire trucks are coming back."

“1...2...3 fire trucks!” I counted as the trucks backed into the firehouse.

“Each truck does a different job,” Uncle Grady explained.

"The rushing water from the pumper truck makes the fire hose jump around," said Uncle Grady. "That is why it takes more than one fire fighter to handle each hose."

"I, Grover, would be a terrific hose handler," I told Uncle Grady. "I always help Mommy water our garden."

My favorite truck was the hook and ladder truck. Uncle Grady said the ladders can reach the windows of tall buildings.

There was a steering wheel in the front of the truck and another one in the back.

"The driver steers the front of the truck. The tiller is the driver who steers the back. That is how we get the hook and ladder truck around corners," said Uncle Grady.

"When I am a fire fighter, can we drive a hook and ladder truck together?" I asked him. He liked that idea.

The fire fighters were very busy. Some of them were washing the fire trucks. Others were checking the hoses for breaks.

"That looks like fun!" I told Uncle Grady.

"It is hard work," he said. "Fire fighters have to be sure their equipment is always ready to go."

When we got home, I told Mommy, "I want to put out fires, and steer a hook and ladder truck, and give baths to fire trucks, and help handle fire hoses.

"When I grow up, I want to be a fire fighter."